Scout
THE DOG WHO SAVED
The Nutcracker

Marilyn Sebesta

Dedication

To Scout's "aunts" and "uncles"
- Nancy, Jane, Charles and Lawrence -
who readily share their time and treats with her

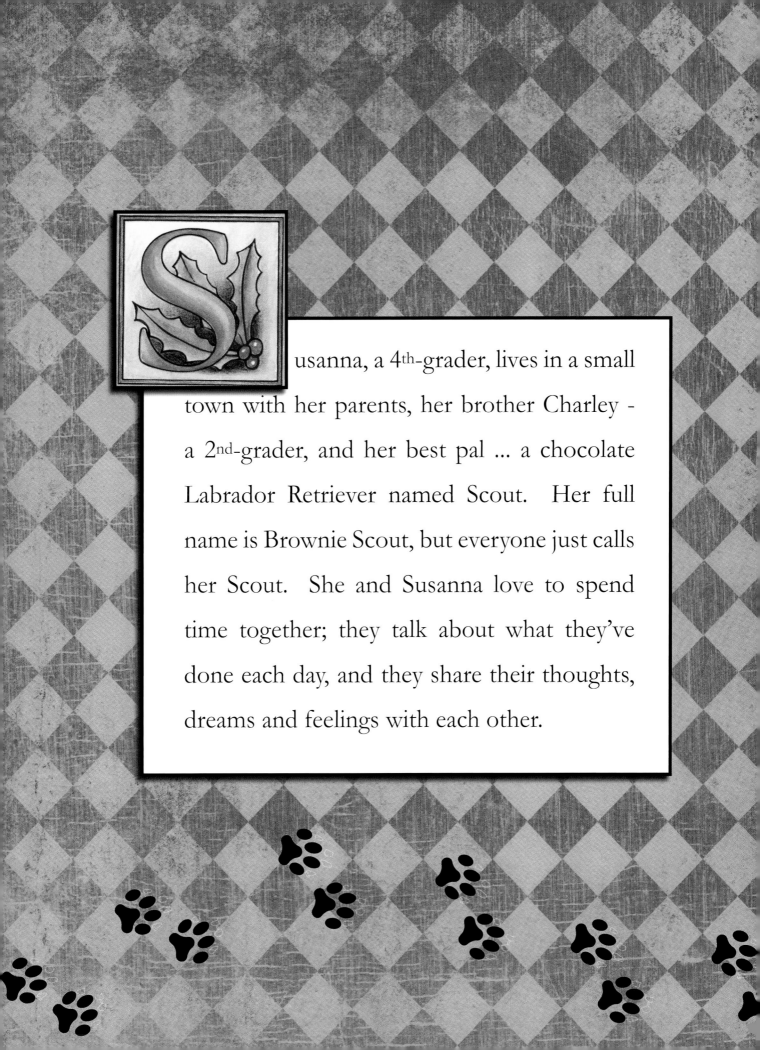

usanna, a 4th-grader, lives in a small town with her parents, her brother Charley - a 2nd-grader, and her best pal ... a chocolate Labrador Retriever named Scout. Her full name is Brownie Scout, but everyone just calls her Scout. She and Susanna love to spend time together; they talk about what they've done each day, and they share their thoughts, dreams and feelings with each other.

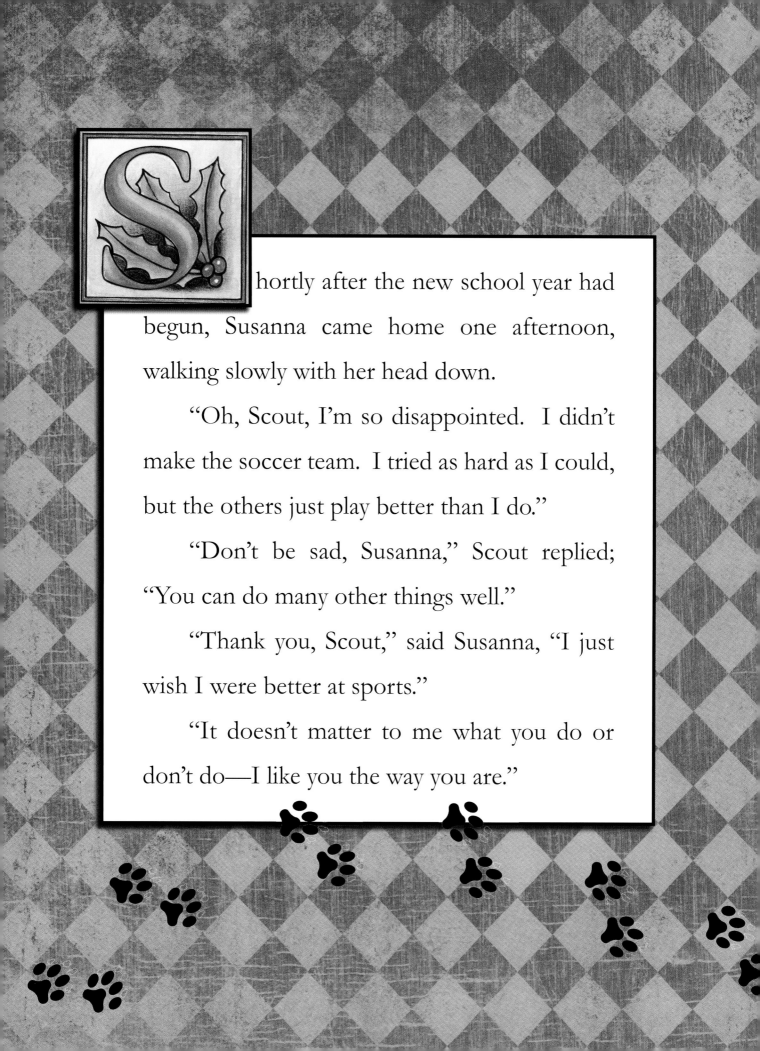

hortly after the new school year had begun, Susanna came home one afternoon, walking slowly with her head down.

"Oh, Scout, I'm so disappointed. I didn't make the soccer team. I tried as hard as I could, but the others just play better than I do."

"Don't be sad, Susanna," Scout replied; "You can do many other things well."

"Thank you, Scout," said Susanna, "I just wish I were better at sports."

"It doesn't matter to me what you do or don't do—I like you the way you are."

hen Susanna arrived home from school the following day, Scout wasn't waiting at the fence as she usually was. Susanna called her name, but she didn't come running to her. Susanna breathlessly ran into her house, exclaiming to her mother, "Scout's gone!"

Her mother was talking on the telephone saying, "We'll be right over to get her."

"Are you talking about Scout?" Susanna asked.

"Yes," her mother answered. "Someone must have opened the gate, and Scout ran across the street to the dance studio. She's fine—the dance students found her name and telephone number on her ID tag, so they knew who to call."

Susanna rushed out of the house with her mother to get Scout. She was relieved to find her playing with the dance students. Several of the students were Susanna's friends, including her best friend Gracie, and they invited her to join their class. Miss Sheila, the dance teacher, came outside at that time to check on her students. She said to Susanna's mother, "I've just started a class in which the students may bring their dogs. The dogs learn to be graceful just like the students. I think it would be really good for Susanna and Scout."

"Oh, please, Mom, may Scout and I join the class?" begged Susanna.

"I think that's a wonderful idea; yes, you may both begin dance lessons," replied Susanna's mother.

That night at supper, Susanna told her dad how excited she was that she and Scout would begin taking dance lessons. He told her that he thought she would be a good dancer and that he looked forward to coming to watch both her and Scout perform.

usanna and Scout went to Miss Sheila's dance studio the next week for their first class. Miss Sheila fitted all the students, including dogs, with tutus and ballet slippers. When she got to Scout, she realized that she didn't have any large enough. The tutu wouldn't fit all the way around her waist, and the largest ballet slippers were still too small.

Miss Sheila said, "I know what we'll do."

"We'll go next door to the feed store and see if Mr. Barker can help us out. He has all sorts of interesting items, and he always has a solution."   Susanna and Scout followed Miss Sheila into Mr. Barker's store.

After hearing what the problem was, Mr. Barker said, "I have just the right solution." He left for a few minutes and came back with a rope. He attached it to both ends of the tutu in order to extend it to fit around Scout's waist. "Let me think," he said, "I know we can come up with some ballet slippers." Then his eyes sparkled as he said, "I have the perfect answer." He went into his office and brought back a set of golf clubs. He removed two of the leather covers that were used to protect the wooden clubs. He said, "I have extra covers at home; I'll be glad to share these with Scout." They didn't look quite like the other ballet slippers, but Scout was proud to have her own special pair of dancing shoes.

Miss Sheila, Susanna and Scout returned to the dance studio where the others were already practicing warm-up exercises. Miss Sheila told the class that the first ballet step they would learn was the pirouette, which is a full turn on the ball of one foot. Susanna and the other students seemed to catch on fast, and they began twirling around and around. The dogs in the class—the Poodles, the Terriers, the Beagles, and the Cocker Spaniels—were having a grand time spinning around.

cout, the only Labrador Retriever, was having a little trouble balancing on just two feet, but she didn't let that stop her from trying. As she tried to make a complete turn, her large otter-like tail hit one of the Poodles and knocked her off her feet. The Poodle was not very happy about that, and neither were the other small dogs. They were afraid they might be next to be hit by Scout's tail.

iss Sheila thought it best to move Scout to the back row where she would have plenty of room to practice her pirouettes. Scout didn't mind being at the back; she was just glad she was a member of the class. Susanna, meanwhile, was showing promise of becoming an exceptionally good ballerina. Scout was slowly improving, although she wasn't nearly as graceful as the other dogs.

As Susanna and Scout were discussing their dance class one day, Susanna told Scout, "Don't be discouraged if you can't move as fast as the other dogs; I like the way you look when you dance in your own way."

The dancers were getting excited about their first performance—"The Nutcracker," a fairy tale-ballet by Tchaikovsky—which they would perform the first weekend of December. They were looking forward to finding out which parts they would have in the production. Susanna was thrilled to learn she had been selected to play the part of Clara. Even Charley and some of his friends joined the dance class because they wanted to act out the parts of soldiers or mice. Since Scout was a little clumsy, Miss Sheila had a hard time deciding which part would be best for her. She thought Scout would be good as Mother Ginger; she wouldn't do much dancing, just sort of sway in a very large skirt. Several small roly-poly clowns were to scamper out from beneath the skirt and perform a dance. Scout was pleased with her character and watched with great interest as Susanna's mother sewed her costume.

A week before "The Nutcracker" was to be performed, Susanna, Scout and Charley went to Mr. Barker's feed store to purchase a new dog collar and some treats for Scout.

Mr. Barker asked, "How is your practice for 'The Nutcracker' going? I'm planning on coming to see your performance."

With pride in her voice, Susanna told him that she was going to be Clara and that Scout was going to be Mother Ginger.

"Guess who I'm going to be, Mr. Barker?" asked Charley.

He thought for a moment and then said, "I'll bet you're going to be a soldier."

"You're right," replied Charley. "I'm going to be a soldier who will help the Nutcracker battle the Mouse King."

nknown to Mr. Barker, Susanna, Charley and Scout, the mice that lived at the feed store were listening to the conversation. "A king? Does he mean that we actually have our own king?" chattered the mice. "I sure hope we get to see him when he comes here."

As Susanna, Scout and Charley left the feed store, Scout spotted the mice and waved good-bye to them. Scout liked everybody—she didn't care how big or small they were or what they looked like.

After they left, the mice performed their own little dance, chanting to each other, "We want to see the king!"

he big weekend finally arrived! Miss Sheila told the class that they would have their final rehearsal, complete with costumes, on Friday evening. The dancers would perform for the public on Saturday evening. Susanna's parents helped get her, Charley and Scout dressed in their new costumes and took pictures of them to send to their relatives who lived too far away to come to the performance. They walked with them to the high school auditorium, which was a block from their house. The parents said they would be back in two hours to walk them home.

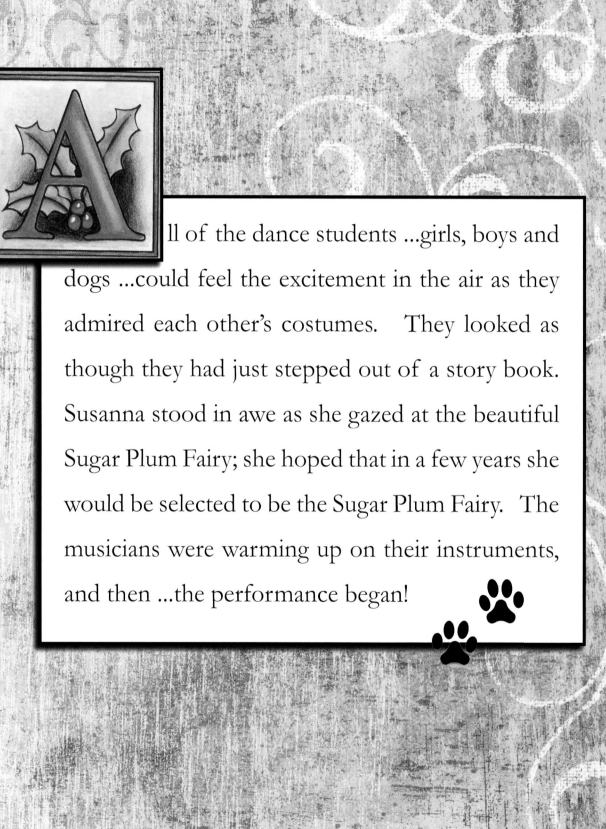

All of the dance students …girls, boys and dogs …could feel the excitement in the air as they admired each other's costumes.   They looked as though they had just stepped out of a story book. Susanna stood in awe as she gazed at the beautiful Sugar Plum Fairy; she hoped that in a few years she would be selected to be the Sugar Plum Fairy.   The musicians were warming up on their instruments, and then …the performance began!

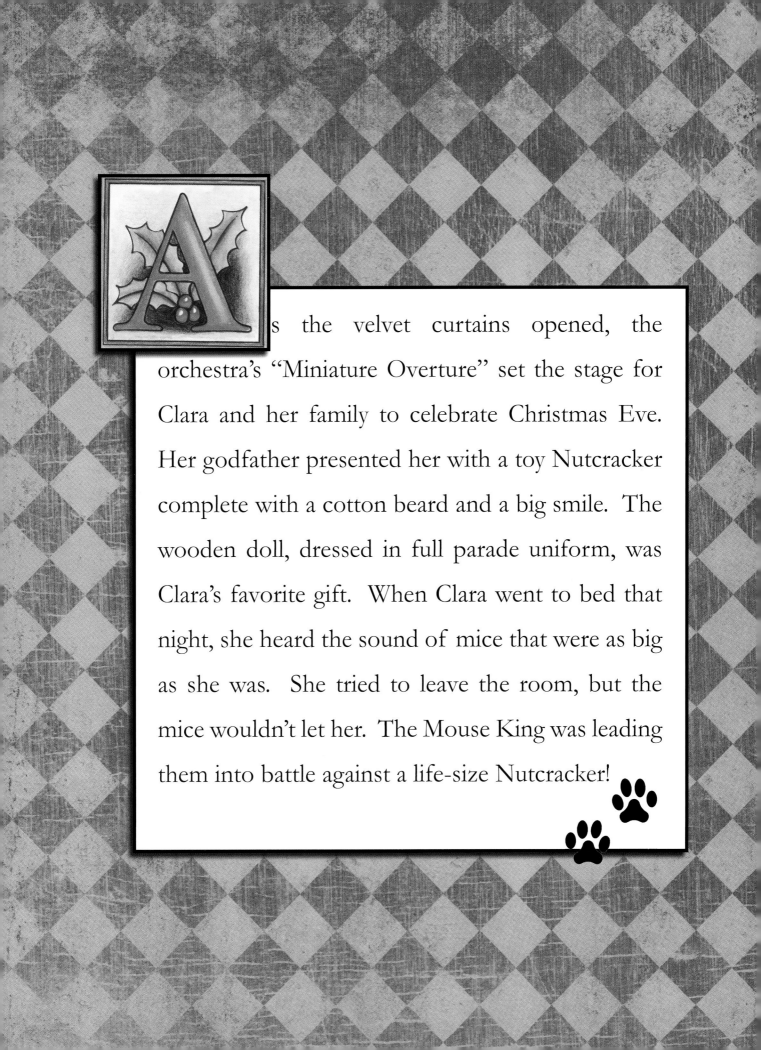

As the velvet curtains opened, the orchestra's "Miniature Overture" set the stage for Clara and her family to celebrate Christmas Eve. Her godfather presented her with a toy Nutcracker complete with a cotton beard and a big smile. The wooden doll, dressed in full parade uniform, was Clara's favorite gift. When Clara went to bed that night, she heard the sound of mice that were as big as she was. She tried to leave the room, but the mice wouldn't let her. The Mouse King was leading them into battle against a life-size Nutcracker!

ith so much excitement, nobody noticed the real-life mice crawling in through the back stage door.

When the dancers saw the mice on the stage, the girls began to scream, the small dogs began to faint and the boys went outside to look for any available cats! Everything was in total confusion! Miss Sheila didn't like the mice, either; she jumped on a table at the side of the stage. Scout recognized the mice as her friends from Mr. Barker's feed store. With her tail wagging, she ran over to them.

She said, "Hey, buddies—welcome to our performance."

They responded in unison, "We want to see the Mouse King!" Scout could see that it was up to her to save the show.

She replied, "I know of something you might want more than seeing the Mouse King."

"What's that?" asked the mice.

Scout said, "Today when I was walking behind the feed store, I saw a farmer loading a sack of corn in his pickup. The sack slipped out of his hands and tore, leaving all the corn on the ground."

orn? Did you say 'corn'? We haven't had any corn since last summer," the mice exclaimed.

"Just follow me ...I'll take you right to it," said Scout. In Pied Piper-fashion, Scout led the happy mice off the stage, out the back door, down the street and on to where the pile of corn was.

"Oh, Scout ...thank you, thank you," said the mice. "We'd much rather be given corn than to see *anybody*, including the Mouse King. We won't even think about going back to see 'The Nutcracker.' We have work to do; we need to divide and store this corn so it will last our families all winter."

cout hurried back to the high school auditorium as fast as her large skirt would allow her to go. As she came through the back door, the dancers were slowly getting back on their feet, trying to resume the performance.

"It's Scout!" shouted the dancers. "She's the one who saved the show." They all ran to thank her and to hug her.

Miss Sheila came down from the table and said to the dancers, "In recognition of Scout's quick-thinking bravery, I'm going to change her name. Since she's a chocolate Lab, her name will be changed from 'Mother Ginger' to 'Mother Mocha.' She will be our honored guest for the rest of this rehearsal and for tomorrow's performance. She will sit on the stage with Clara and the Prince and watch the dances with them."

All the dancers cheered, "Scout's our hero!"

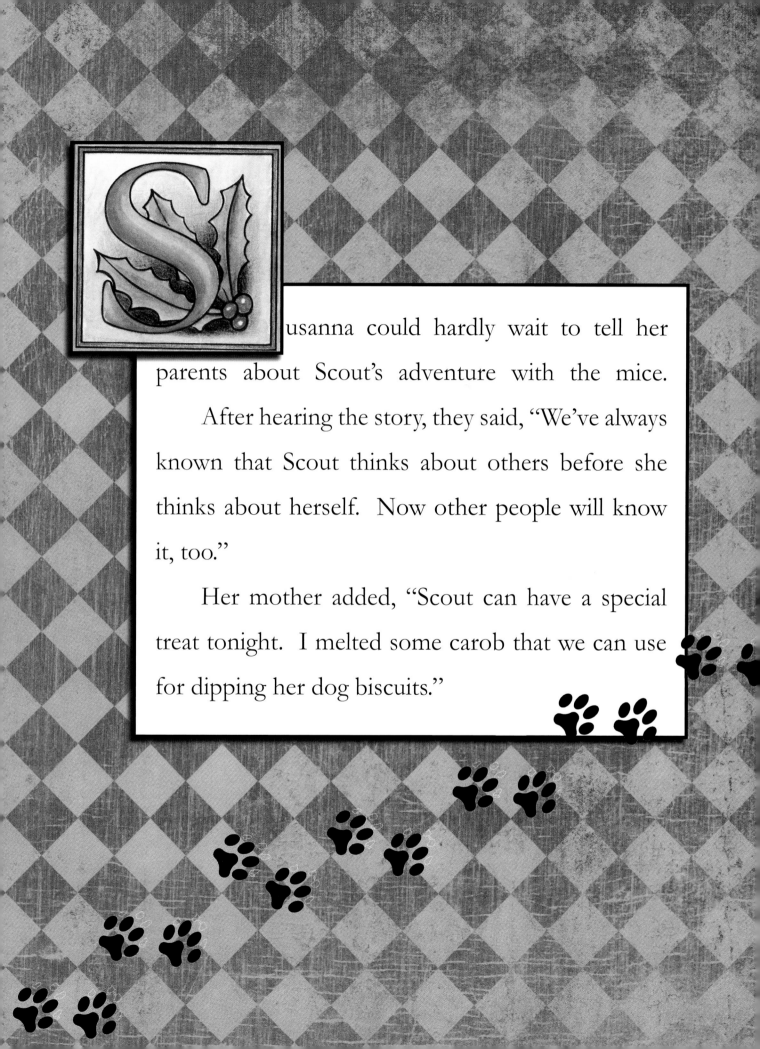

usanna could hardly wait to tell her parents about Scout's adventure with the mice.

After hearing the story, they said, "We've always known that Scout thinks about others before she thinks about herself. Now other people will know it, too."

Her mother added, "Scout can have a special treat tonight. I melted some carob that we can use for dipping her dog biscuits."

cout and Susanna were too happy and excited to go to sleep. After Susanna's parents and Charley had fallen asleep, she and Scout got out of bed and went into the kitchen. They wanted to share their joy with everybody in the performance ...girls, boys, dogs and musicians ...by making treats for them. For the dogs, they dipped enough dog biscuits in melted carob so that each dog could have one. For the others in the performance, they prepared Holiday Popcorn Delight. They made individual packages and labeled them "Nutcracker Sweets."

The opening night ...an event all the dance students had been looking forward to ...was finally here! The high school auditorium was packed with every seat taken. A sign that read "SRO" (Standing Room Only) had been placed on the front door.

The dance students knew their lines and dances perfectly. They came to the part where Clara threw her shoe at the Mouse King, and the life-size Nutcracker stabbed the Mouse King. At that point, the Nutcracker was transformed into a Prince. He took Clara's hand as a light snow began to fall. The Snowflakes began to dance, leading Clara and the Prince to his palace in the Land of Sweets.

other Mocha was already sitting on the Throne of Delight waiting for Clara and the Prince to take their places with her. What sights they saw! There were cakes, ice cream sundaes and chocolate bonbons. The beautiful Sugar Plum Fairy and the people of the Land of Sweets danced for the three honored guests. Dancers included Spanish Hot Chocolate, Arabian Coffee, Chinese Tea, Candy Canes, and Flowers that glided, spun, flew, whirled and leaped across the stage.

The roly-poly clowns made their way to the throne and said to Mother Mocha, "Thank you for your fine example of courage. Now we're not afraid to dance right out on the stage; we no longer have to hide under your skirt!"

he Sugar Plum Fairy and her Cavalier gracefully performed a dance before she called all the Delights together for a final dance of celebration in honor of the Prince, Clara and Mother Mocha.

he Sugar Plum Fairy invited them down from their throne and again praised them for their bravery. She hugged each of them and then ushered them to their waiting sleigh. The curtains closed as Mother Mocha, Clara and the Prince waved goodbye to the dancers and the audience. The crowd rose to their feet, cheering and applauding all the performers.

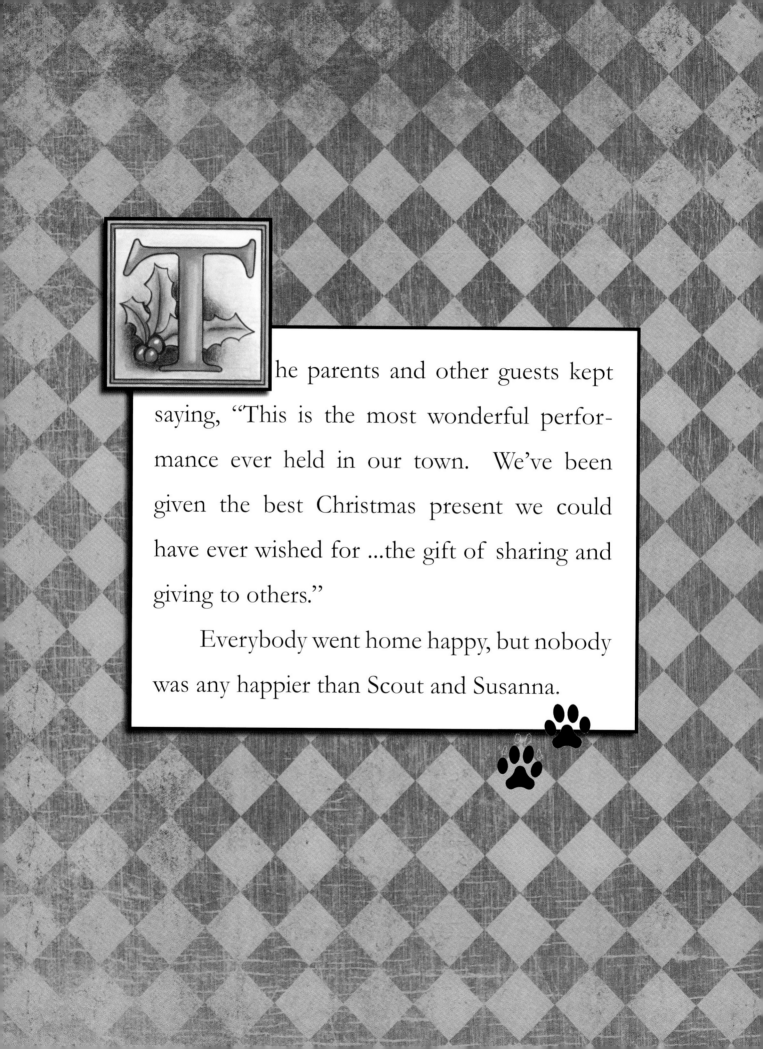

The parents and other guests kept saying, "This is the most wonderful performance ever held in our town. We've been given the best Christmas present we could have ever wished for ...the gift of sharing and giving to others."

Everybody went home happy, but nobody was any happier than Scout and Susanna.

Nutcracker SCOUT'S Sweets

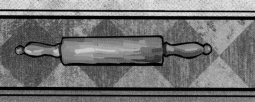

SUGAR PLUM FAIRY'S SUGAR KISSES

1 (16-ounce) roll refrigerated sugar cookie dough
24 foil-wrapped chocolate candy kisses
1 cup pecans (ground or chopped in small pieces)

1. Preheat oven to 350º.
2. Divide cookie dough into 24 equal pieces; roll each piece into a small ball.
3. Roll each ball in pecans to completely coat it.
4. Place balls on ungreased cookie sheets.
5. Bake for 12 to 14 minutes or until cookies begin to turn golden; remove from oven.
6. Immediately press unwrapped candy kiss in center of each cookie.
7. Place cookies on wire rack to cool; do not stack until completely cool.

MOTHER MOCHA'S HOT CHOCOLATE MIX

1 (25.6-ounce) box nonfat dry milk powder
1 (16-ounce) box powdered sugar
1 (16-ounce) container instant chocolate mix
1 (11-ounce) jar nondairy coffee creamer

1. Combine all ingredients; mix well to smooth out any sugar lumps.
2. Store in an airtight container.
3. To serve, put ¼ cup mix in a cup; fill with 8 ounces of hot water.
4. **Optional**: May add one of the following to dry mix in cup before filling it with hot water:
   - 1 teaspoon crushed peppermint candy discs
   - ¼ teaspoon instant coffee crystals
5. Makes about 18 cups of dry mix (72 cups of hot chocolate).

SCOUT'S DIPPED DOGGIE TREATS

For Your Favorite Pooch

1/4 cup carob chips (Do **not** substitute chocolate chips!)
Tiny amount of cooking oil
Dog biscuit treats (purchased)
Chicken and/or beef bouillon granules

1. Microwave carob chips in a small microwave-safe dish for 1 minute at half power -or - 30 seconds at full power or until chips are melted.
2. Remove from microwave; add a tiny amount of cooking oil and stir chips until mixture is smooth.
3. Holding the dog treat in one hand, spoon the mixture on other end of treat to cover about 1 inch; it may be dipped if mixture isn't too thick.
4. Roll dipped end in chicken or beef bouillon granules and place on waxed paper to dry. (Treats may also be left plain.)
5. Store in a closed container in a cool place.
6. Makes about 8 medium dog biscuit treats.

LAND OF SWEETS GUMDROP BARS

2 cups biscuit mix
1 (16-ounce) box light brown sugar
1 cup chopped candy gumdrops (approximately 48)
1 teaspoon vanilla
4 eggs, well beaten

1. Preheat oven to 350º.
2. Grease and flour (or spray) a 9-inch by 13-inch cake pan to keep bar cookies from sticking.
3. Stir biscuit mix and brown sugar together; add chopped gumdrops.
4. Mix in well beaten eggs and vanilla.
5. Pour into pan.
6. Bake for about 30 to 35 minutes or until edges come loose from pan and center is set.
7. After cookies are cool, cut into 24 squares.
8. Note: *These chewy bar cookies are generally higher at the edges than in the center of the pan, so don't think they have fallen. They're meant to be that way!*

Susanna's Holiday Popcorn Delight

16 cups caramel-coated popcorn (purchased)
1 cup semi-sweet chocolate chunks or chips
1 cup small red & green candy-coated milk chocolate candies
1 cup roasted/salted almonds
1 cup roasted/salted peanuts (optional)
1 cup dried cranberries
1 cup golden raisins

Mix all ingredients together in a large bowl;
makes approximately 18 one-cup servings.

Prince's Crown Jewel Clusters

16 ounces white chocolate, melted
1 cup broken pretzel sticks
1 cup toasted rice cereal
1 cup miniature marshmallows
1 cup chopped pecans
1 cup small multi-colored candy-coated milk chocolate candies

1. Melt white chocolate in microwave or on stove top according to package directions.
2. Add all other ingredients; stir until blended.
3. Drop by spoonfuls onto cookie sheet lined with waxed paper.
4. Place clusters in refrigerator to harden. Store in cool place in covered container. (The refrigerator is the best place, especially in summer.)
5. Makes approximately 3 dozen (2-inch) clusters.